Fairy Tale Fixers

Fixing Fairy Tale Problems with STEM

THE PRINCESS AND THE PEA

Pass the Pea Pressure Test!

Jasmine Brooke

Gareth Stevens
PUBLISHING

Please visit our website, www.garethstevens.com.
For a free color catalog of all our high-quality books,
call toll free 1-800-542-2595 or fax 1-877-542-2596.

Cataloging-in-Publication Data
Names: Brooke, Jasmine.
Title: The princess and the pea: pass the pea pressure test! / Jasmine Brooke.
Description: New York : Gareth Stevens Publishing, 2018. | Series: Fairy tale fixers: fixing fairy tale
    problems with STEM | Includes index.
Identifiers: ISBN 9781538206782 (pbk.) | ISBN 9781538206751 (library bound) | ISBN 9781538206676
    (6 pack)
Subjects: LCSH: Fairy tales--Adaptations--Juvenile fiction. | Princesses--Juvenile fiction. | Peas--Juvenile
    fiction. | Simple machines--Juvenile fiction. | Engineering--Fiction.
Classification: LCC PZ7.B766 Pri 2018 | DDC [E]--dc23

First Edition

Published in 2018 by
Gareth Stevens Publishing
111 East 14th Street, Suite 349
New York, NY 10003

Copyright © 2018 Gareth Stevens Publishing

Produced for Gareth Stevens by Calcium
Editors: Sarah Eason and Harriet McGregor
Designer: Paul Myerscough
Illustrators: David Pavon and Anita Romeo
Consultant: David Hawksett

Printed in the United States of America

CPSIA compliance information: Batch #CS17GS
For further information contact Gareth Stevens, New York, New York at 1-800-542-2595.

CONTENTS

How to Use This Book

How do you know if a princess really is a princess? You use a little STEM-thinking! Read the story, try out some fun experiments, and use your STEM skills to figure out innovative ways to fix fairy tale problems! Then look for the STEM solutions on page 30 to see if your experiment conclusions are right.

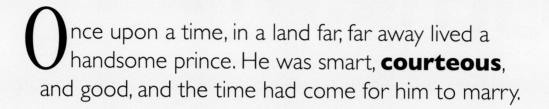

Once upon a time, in a land far, far away lived a handsome prince. He was smart, **courteous**, and good, and the time had come for him to marry.

The king and queen introduced their son to beautiful princesses from far and wide. He met princesses from the West and princesses from the East. He danced with princesses from the North and princesses from the South. Some princesses were funny. Others were kind. Some had great talents. Each would make a wonderful queen. But the prince liked none of them. "Only a perfect princess will do," he told the king and queen.

4

6

To find his perfect princess, the prince set off on a great journey that took him all over the world.

The prince traveled to many wonderful kingdoms. He traveled to the lands of sweeping desert, with majestic castles surrounded by beautiful gardens. He traveled to kingdoms of snow and ice, where he rode in a carriage pulled by great wolves. He traveled to the lands of towering mountains and to kingdoms where the ocean crashed against castles that clung to the cliffs.

In all these places, he met beautiful princesses, but none of them was perfect. So the prince came home again and was unhappy because he did so want to marry a perfect princess.

Years passed and still the prince had not married. The king and queen worried that their son would never find true happiness. Everyone in the kingdom talked about when the lonely prince would finally find a bride. "When will our son have a family of his own to ensure the future of the kingdom?" sobbed the queen.

One evening, a terrible storm blew up around the castle. Lightning burst across the sky. Thunder boomed through the air. Rain poured from the heavens and soaked the ground below. It was truly terrifying to see and hear.

As they gathered in the Great Hall by the fire, the king and queen heard a knock at the castle gate. "Whoever is out in this terrible weather?" the queen cried. The king hurried to the gate and opened it.

As the gate opened, the king gasped in surprise. Who should be standing outside but a beautiful young woman, and what a sight she was in all that rain and wind! Water streamed from her hair, down her clothes, and into her shoes. It even ran out at the heels! The young woman was completely soaked with rain from head to toe. She was quite frozen with the cold and pale from her **ordeal** in the storm.

"Come inside, come inside!" **ushered** the king, pulling the girl into the castle and out of the pouring rain. "You will catch your death in this terrible storm."

The king and queen led the girl to the fireside, where she warmed herself in the heat. "Who are you?" the queen asked her, intrigued by the mysterious stranger. "I am a princess!" the beautiful young woman replied.

The queen was amazed to hear the princess's claim. "We'll soon find out," she told herself, refusing to believe that a real princess would be out in a storm, wandering in the dark.

"We must get you warm and dry," the queen told the girl. "And then safely into bed." The queen told her servants to prepare a bedchamber at once. "Make up the bed," she ordered. "But we must have at least 20 mattresses — the bed must be as soft as a feather for our princess guest."

The servants made up the bed, just as the queen had instructed. Then, when they had finished, she ushered them from the room. Alone, she took a pea she had hidden inside her pocket and placed it under the mattress at the bottom of the bed.

pea PRESSURE TEST

Can a pea really take the **pressure** of 20 mattresses? Before she tested the princess, perhaps the queen should first have tested her pea!

The servants made up the bed, just as the queen had instructed. . . she took a pea she had inside her pocket, placed it under the mattresses, and hopped on top.

Queen: "Let's see how my pea responds to the pressure, before I test our princess. Time for a STEM snooze!"

You Will Need

- Four frozen peas
- Four thawed peas
- Paper towel
- Deck of cards weighing around 8 ounces (225 g)
- Four books each weighing around 6 ounces (170 g)
- Plastic princess toy weighing around 4 ounces (115 g)
- Notepad and pen

Help the queen carry out her pea pressure test!

1 Place a sheet of paper towel on a hard surface that is at eye level. Then arrange your four thawed peas in a square.

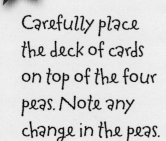

2 Carefully place the deck of cards on top of the four peas. Note any change in the peas.

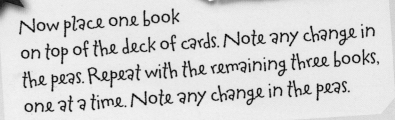

3 Now place one book on top of the deck of cards. Note any change in the peas. Repeat with the remaining three books, one at a time. Note any change in the peas.

14

4 Finally, place your figurine on top of the books. Note any change in the peas. Take off all the books and cards and note what has happened to the peas. Did they maintain their shape?

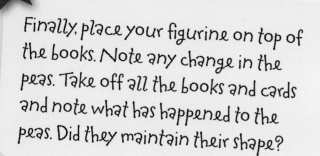

5 Now repeat the entire experiment again, but this time with four frozen peas. Note how the peas respond at each stage. What is the difference between the frozen and thawed peas?

innovate!

Compare how the frozen peas perform against frozen foods that are larger. For example, compare pieces of frozen raspberries with the frozen peas. Do the larger food pieces maintain their shape better under pressure? Why do you think that is so? Note your conclusion, and then turn to the STEM Solutions on page 30 to see if you are right.

With the pea safely hidden beneath the mattresses, the queen led the young woman into the bedchamber. "Here you are, my dear," she told her. "Now, you must rest. I will return in the morning to see how you have slept."

Bidding the princess good night, the queen left the bedchamber and locked the door behind her. She smiled at her plan and said to herself, "Only a real princess will feel that pea beneath the mattresses. I'll wager that she sleeps through the night and never notices a thing!"

As the queen took to her own bedchamber, the king told her, "Imagine that, a princess in the rain! Well, perhaps this storm will bring some good fortune to our lives." The queen merely smiled and said, "Do not trouble yourself, my dear. I am sure all will reveal itself in good time."

In the morning, the queen returned to the young woman's bedchamber. "Well, my dear," she smiled, "did you sleep well?"

"Oh, thank you for asking!" said the girl. "But I am sorry to say that I scarcely slept at all. I lay on something so hard that I am black and blue all over. I could not rest. It was simply terrible." She rubbed at her back and legs, and the queen could see for herself that her skin was indeed bruised.

Amazed, the queen stared at the young woman. She could hardly believe that she had really felt the pea beneath the 20 mattresses!

The queen embraced the girl. To have felt one pea all the way through 20 mattresses, she must be a real princess, without doubt. Nobody but a princess could be so delicate.

"You must truly be a princess," the queen gasped. "Only a princess could feel such a thing."

She lifted the mattress at the bottom of the bed and showed the young woman the pea that she had placed there. "I could not believe that you really were a princess," the queen confessed. "So I decided to test you by placing the pea in the bed. But I can now see that you are of royal blood, and there can be no question about it."

TEST THE MATTRESS

Could the firmness of the mattresses have affected how much the princess felt the pea? Perhaps the queen should have applied another STEM test!

To have felt one pea all the way through 20 mattresses. . . she must be a real princess, or. . .
Queen: "A princess, bah! A peasant would have felt a pea through those worn old mattresses!"

Use your STEM skills to discover which type of material makes the firmest mattress.

1 Tear off a paper towel sheet, scrunch it up, and stuff it into your first bag. Continue to do this until your bag is full.

2 Tie the bag shut.

3 Cut up strips of fabric, and stuff the second bag as full as you can. Tie the bag shut.

22

4

Stuff your third bag with cotton balls and tie the bag shut.

5

Place a heavy book on each mattress and press down on it.

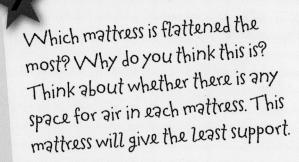

6

Which mattress keeps its shape the best? (Note: this is the mattress that does not easily squash down.) This mattress will give the most **support**.

7

Which mattress is flattened the most? Why do you think this is? Think about whether there is any space for air in each mattress. This mattress will give the least support.

innovate!

Try filling your mattress with other materials. Use feathers, sawdust, or sand. Which of these materials makes the firmest mattress? Why is this? Note your conclusion, and then turn to the STEM Solutions on page 30 to see if you are right.

23

With the joyful news, the queen led the princess to the king. She explained to him that only a princess of the purest royal blood could feel a pea beneath so many layers. "She is truly precious," the queen announced. "We must introduce her at once to our son. At last, here is a princess beyond compare."

The king hurried to bring his son to meet the princess, and as soon as he saw the young woman, the prince fell immediately in love. There before him stood the most perfect princess — beautiful, smart, and of the purest royal blood. He had traveled the world for years to find a perfect princess bride, yet just one stormy night had delivered him the prize of which he dreamed.

The prince immediately decided to make the princess his bride. The king and queen sent messengers across the kingdom to tell all their subjects of their good fortune. At last, their son had found his perfect princess bride and the future of the kingdom would now be secure.

In the grandeur of the castle, the prince and princess wed before the king, queen, and the **nobles** of the land. All bowed before the prince and his most beautiful princess wife.

And forever after, their story became known as that of the "princess and the pea."

make a PULLEY

The poor princess would have needed a ladder to climb the 20 mattresses! A simple **pulley** could have fixed her fairy tale problem!

You Will Need

- Twine or string
- Two hooks, like on the back of a bedroom door (If you do not have hooks, ask an adult to hammer two nails into a piece of wood or a wall.)
- Three small carabiners
- Princess doll
- Notepad and pen

Bidding the princess good night, the queen left the bedchamber and locked the door behind her.
Princess: "Only a pea-brained princess would climb that mattress tower. Pulley-power and STEM will propel me to the top!"

Use your **engineering** skills to make a pulley for the princess!

1 Cut a long piece of twine. It needs to be long enough to reach from your hooks to the ground at least three times.

2 Tie one end of the twine to a carabiner.

3 Hook the carabiner over the first hook.

4 Place the second carabiner over the second hook.

28

5 Pass the twine through the second carabiner.

6 Slot the princess doll's arm through the third carabiner.

7 Attach this carabiner to the piece of twine between the two hooks.

8 Pull the free end of the twine down to lift up the princess.

innovate!

Try lifting a heavier object both with and without the pulley. Does the pulley make it easier? Note your conclusion, and then turn to the STEM Solutions on page 30 to see if you are right.

29

STEM SOLUTIONS

Pea Pressure Test

Water makes up 90 percent of vegetables. When a pea is frozen, the water in its **cells** becomes ice. That makes the frozen pea harder and more able to **resist** pressure, such as a weight bearing down on it. However, as water becomes ice, it **expands**. The ice pushes against the cell walls of the pea and starts to break them.

When the pea thaws, the frozen water, or ice, turns back into water. Because the cell walls of the pea were damaged during the freezing process, the thawed pea is a much softer, mushier structure than it was before it was frozen. As a frozen object, the pea was much stronger and could resist pressure. As a thawed object, the pea was much weaker and was more easily squashed.

Test the Mattress

The mattress that contained strips of fabric kept its shape the best. The mattress that contained paper towels flattened most easily. In each mattress, the filling took up some space and air filled the remainder. The more air pockets in the mattress, the more easily the mattress could be flattened.

It is difficult to remove the air pockets in a feather mattress when you press down on it. For that reason, feathers would have made a soft mattress. To make a firm mattress, you could have used sawdust or sand. Both can be packed close together, to remove air pockets between them.

Make a Pulley

The use of a pulley changes the direction of the **force** needed to lift an object. You pulled down on the rope to lift up the princess doll. The princess doll was also **suspended** from two points. Her weight was split equally between the two points. That meant that you needed to pull with only half as much force to lift her than you would have used if she was suspended from one point. However, you did have to pull the rope twice as far to lift up the doll.

FURTHER READING

Books

Andrews, Beth. *Hands-On Engineering.* Waco, TX: Prufrock Press, 2012.

Carey, Anne. *STEAM Kids: 50+ Science / Technology / Engineering / Art / Math Hands-On Projects for Kids.* CreateSpace Independent Publishing, 2016.

Colfer, Chris. *The Land of Stories: A Treasury of Classic Fairy Tales.* New York, NY: Little, Brown, 2016.

Frinkle, Andrew. *50 Stem Labs — Science Experiments for Kids.* CreateSpace Independent Publishing, 2014.

Websites

Check out the fun science activities at:
www.kineticcity.com

Find out how pulleys and other devices work at:
science.howstuffworks.com/transport/engines-equipment/pulley.htm

Try out fun science experiments at:
www.sciencebuddies.org

Discover even more great STEM ideas at:
stem-works.com

Publisher's note to educators and parents: Our editors have carefully reviewed these websites to ensure that they are suitable for students. Many websites change frequently, however, and we cannot guarantee that a site's future contents will continue to meet our high standards of quality and educational value. Be advised that students should be closely supervised whenever they access the Internet.

GLOSSARY

carabiner a device used to attach ropes to other objects

cells smallest parts of living things

courteous having good manners

engineering using mathematical and technical skills to build things or find solutions to problems

expands gets bigger

force a push or pulling action

nobles important people who helped advise kings and queens

ordeal a terrible experience

pressure a force applied with weight

pulley a device that makes it easier to lift heavy objects

resist to not give in

support to hold something up

suspended held up in the air

thawed no longer frozen

ushered ordered into a place

INDEX